# ALIEN ABDUCTION FOR SANTA

## THE INTERGALACTIC GUIDE TO HUMANS

SKYE MACKINNON

Peryton Press

# CONTENTS

# LESSON 1

# HOW TO FIND A MOVING TARGET

My skin flashes bright green as I stare at the man on the screen.

"It's him!" my sister cheers, her colouring changing just as rapidly as my own. "Finally."

We've been looking for him for over a week, but now our scanners have finally found him. Our future mate.

I take him in, all six feet of humanness. I don't want to be called speciesist, but humans are one of the sexiest aliens out there. Karangi may come close, although I think their reputation for beauty is exaggerated. This male, however, is truly stunning. His long red coat highlights his white hair and beard. His coal-black eyes are hidden beneath bushy grey eyebrows that almost seem like tiny lifeforms clinging to his face. His nose is strong with wide nostrils begging to be touched. He'll be a pleasure to kunik with.

He's surprisingly tall for a human, although he'd barely reach my chin. And soon he will. I'll have him pressed against my chest...

"A-Vay, focus," my sister snaps. "Set a new course. Let's get to his location before he moves again. This male is slipperier than a walmop."

She's right about that. Our sensors are top range, yet whenever we thought we'd spotted him, he was gone by the time we had a fix on his whereabouts. He moves fast, faster than their primitive human vehicles should allow. His vehicle is made from a native material they call wood, but we've not been able to find any details on why this *wood* would be superior to more advanced technologies.

My six fingers dance over the keyboard, changing our spaceship's trajectory. A-Ven prefers to use voice control, but I'm old-fashioned. I like to touch things.

I wonder what our human will feel like beneath my finger pads. I'm sure he'll be soft. Squishy. I'll be able to...

"Focus," A-Ven hisses, clearly knowing that I'm dreaming again. She knows me better than any other being in the universe. We shared the same egg and sometimes, it feels like we share the same mind, too.

I push away all thoughts of how our future mate's beard might feel when it brushes against my face and concentrate on our ship's controls. Our target male is far away from civilisation now, making it easy to intercept him. We don't want to break the rules by showing ourselves to the locals, but I'm also desperate to finally catch him. He won't slip through our fingers this time.

"Stealth mode engaged," I mutter as we enter the atmosphere. "I'll park us a short way from his dwelling, then we can walk the remaining bit. I don't want to alert him to our presence."

"Good thinking, sis. Let's be stealthy like our ship."

A-Ven turns to the fabricator and scrolls through a list of local garments. We've been scanning Peritus long enough to find out what native females like to wear. It seems to vary a lot between regions, so I take a quick look at the weather conditions at our destination.

"Make it something loose and airy," I tell my sister. "It's almost four hundred glyptons there. That's positively scorching."

"Let's not stay there for too long or my skin will melt. I hate hot climates. Why couldn't he have chosen somewhere colder to live?"

"Trust me, we're lucky he's in that part of the planet. There are much hotter areas. We'd need survival suits to even leave our ship."

A-Ven shudders. "And that's why I prefer to be in a spaceship with good air-con. How long till landing?"

"Almost there. Better sit down, the ground here is covered in frozen liquid. I'm not sure how our landing gear will cope with that."

My sister takes the seat next to mine - we had the ship modified to have two captain's chairs - and straps in. I know she trusts me to give us the smoothest landing possible, but we've both got enough experience with travelling to strange planets to know that physics can work differently than we're used to. Before we decided to become approved abductors, we were traders. After years of travelling the galaxy, we got a little bored though without having anyone around. We tried giving hitchhikers a lift, but they rarely wanted to stay for long and always fussed around with their towels. Then we abducted our first male, only to find out it was an infertile female. We dropped her off at the nearest space station, where A-Ven saw the advert for the Intergalactic University.

Thirty lectures and four assignments later, only one abduction stands between us and a degree in Alien Abduction. And because both of us are high-achievers, we went for the most powerful male on the entire planet. We scanned their news and one male kept popping up around the world. His name varies depending on the local language, but his outer appearance doesn't change much. I can't wait to see what he hides under his long, red coat! I hope he's as packed there as his strange vehicle always is. He transports a lot of bags from one place to another, but we've not quite figured out why he does it himself. He's so powerful and well-known, why doesn't he have servants? Even the poorest male back on Ank wouldn't be seen doing hard manual labour like that. At least it should have given him excellent muscle mass. I do like males who can pin me down...

"A-Vay!"

"Sorry, sis. Landing in three...two...one..."

A LOUD CRACK in the frozen liquid beneath us signals our arrival. Our ship groans and leans to one side ever so slightly, but then everything grows silent again, leaving only the hum of the machines as they shut down one by one.

I get dressed into a strange fluffy outfit that A-Ven has prepared. It's bulging all around me like a fat suit. I look at my twin sister, using her as a mirror. We look ridiculous. We usually prefer formfitting clothes that only cover our breasts and bums, but this is the complete opposite.

"Pull up your hood," she suggests. "It's like shutting out the world."

I do as she says, and my world turns cosy. The hood is lined with hair. I wonder if it's of human origin. Us Ankanis don't have body hair. Not that I mind. I've seen from our hitchhikers how much effort it is to keep hair and fur in order. Our target, however, has enough body hair for all three of us.

As soon as we step outside, I want to take off my clothes. It's too hot to wear more than just the bare minimum. There's a slight breeze, but it's not enough to keep us cool.

"This was a bad idea," A-Ven mutters and fans herself. "We should have waited until he travelled to a colder region."

The air here is strange. It's filled with white fluffy things that dance in the wind. Are those animals? A higher intelligence?

I pull out my Planelyser™ and point it at the fluff.

"Crystallised hydrogen-oxygen," it tells us. "The locals call it snow."

"Is it edible?" I ask.

"It's not harmful to Ankanis, but it also offers no nutritional value."

I shrug and hold out my hand, catching some of the

*snow*. It disappears as soon as it hits my skin, turning into liquid.

"Look! It changed shape! It's a shifter!"

I want to jump up and down in excitement. While in orbit around Peritus, I read some of the planet's most popular literature. Again and again, I came across so-called *shifters*; beings that could change from one form to another. They sounded a lot like the extinct Mondians, who could turn into fearsome furry beasts. Sadly, that species died out long before A-Ven and I hatched from our egg, so Peritus might be the only place we'd ever get to see shifters.

"I think they're a little too small for that," A-Ven says mildly. "Shall we find our target before we melt just like this *snow*?"

"Always the serious one," I huff. "But alright then. Let's find Santa."

# LESSON 2

# HOW TO ABDUCT AN UNWILLING MALE

**B**y the time we finally reach our target's dwelling, I'm ready to rip off my clothes. It's too hot on this planet. I think I made a mistake when choosing our costumes. They're making it worse. Maybe something the natives call a *bikini* would have been better. It's similar to what we'd normally wear on Ank, except that a bikini is made from even less fabric. It looks as if a human started to make a proper Ankani outfit and then ran out of material.

Four large beasts stand around the building, grazing on snow. Steam rises from their furry bodies as if they're too hot as well. They have strange appendages growing from their foreheads, reminding me of tree branches. Strange colourful balls hang from the brown appendages, tacky and out of place. I have no idea why anyone would do that to these majestic beasts.

A-Vay points her Planelyser™ at the building.

"One human male," the device announces. "Minimal threat. Watch out for his big sack."

I exchange a look with my sister. "Big sack sounds promising," I smirk. "Although I'm sure the Planelyser™ doesn't mean what I want it to mean."

A-Vay laughs. "We'll find out about his big sack soon enough. Once we have him on board, we can start with the probing. Do you have the tranquiliser?"

I nod and pat my pocket. That's the only good thing about these ridiculous sweatsuits: lots of pockets.

"We can use his vehicle to get him to our ship," my sister suggests and points at the strange vehicle that we've already seen on video. It doesn't have a roof, probably to keep Santa nice and cool. It's made from native trees, but we've seen it fly through the air like a hovercar, so there must be some hidden technology inside that our scanner can't recognise.

"This is called a sledge," the Planelyser™ pipes up. A-Vay has accidentally directed it at the vehicle. "An ancient method of transportation. It has no engine but relies on being pulled by animals like dogs."

I nod towards the brown beasts. "Are those dogs?"

"They are called reindeer," the device answers and I can't help but feel it likes correcting me. "Two females, two males. Medium threat. Watch out for the antlers."

That must be those appendages. I wonder if they skewer their prey with them. They must be formidable hunters. Certainly not animals I'd expect to be domesticated, but things seem to be very different from Ank on this planet.

"Let's do this," A-Vay says, her voice swinging with excitement. The dark patches around her eyes have grown even darker, a clear sign that she's ready to hunt. I assume my own markings have changed colour as well. Not every Ankani has their markings around their eyes, but everyone in our tribe does. It's been passed through the generations and has become something of our brand. My nestfeeder's bank even has an Ankani man with dark mask-like markings around his eyes as her logo.

I pull out the syringe and grab it tightly. I've practised this several times. It should be easy. We're taller than our target, even though he's got a lot more bulk. We don't quite know how fast humans can move. In their video recordings that we syphoned off their global data network, we've seen everything from flying humans to immortal ones, but I assume that just like us back home they have fictional vids, not just documentaries.

Anyway, it's time to grab ourselves a male.

The house is covered in snow, hiding the roof and only letting a small chimney peek out. Smoke rises from it in lazy curls. I thought humans were advanced enough to use electricity for heat rather than fire, but we're far away from any other dwellings so maybe he's not got that sort of infrastructure yet. That doesn't correlate with his flying vehicle which must be very advanced technology for Peritus standards, but that's something we can ask him about once he's aboard our ship. I can't wait to probe him.

A-Vay scans the house with her Planelyser™.

"One door. Windows are shut. Walls are made of spiced bread. Recommend knocking, unless you want to eat the walls."

One day, I'm going to prove that the Planelyser™ has a sense of humour.

"Edible walls?" A-Vay snorts. "We really are on the

strangest planet I've ever visited. I wonder if our target is edible, too."

"I'll certainly take a nibble." I grin. "You go and knock, I'll stand by the door ready to inject him."

"And you're sure the serum is safe for humans?"

"Everything points to it. If he shows any adverse effects, I've got the antidote in my pocket. But don't worry, the IGU would have told us if the serum wasn't approved for Peritus."

I take my position, pressing myself against the wall next to the door. It smells sweet and spicy, giving me a strange feeling of home and comfort. I understand why our target built his house this way. I'd love being surrounded by this scent all day.

"Ready?" my sister asks and I show her my smallest finger in affirmation.

She knocks on the door and steps back to give me room to attack our target. Almost immediately, the door opens and a male steps out. The male we've been pursuing ever since we reached Peritus.

"Ho, ho, ho," he greets A-Vay. "Are you here to deliver your wishlist in person?"

"My wishlist?" my sister asks, but I don't give them any time for conversation.

I launch myself at the male and press the syringe against his neck. The serum is injected automatically and before he can even blink, he collapses onto the snowy ground.

"Hey, I wanted to know what he means," A-Vay protests.

"You can ask him when we're back on the ship. It might distract him if the probing gets uncomfortable."

"Probing should never be uncomfortable," she chides me. "Not if it's conducted by a professional. Don't let Professor Katila hear you say stuff like that."

I roll my eyes. A-Vay always sticks to the rules. I like to bend them a little.

Just in case, I give our male a quick health check. He seems alright, although I'll make sure during probing. I've downloaded everything I could find about humans to our ship's medical database in preparation. We've agreed that I'm going to look after his physical needs, while my sister will deal with everything else.

"Let's get him back to the ship," I say with a satisfied smile. "We've got some probing to do."

# LESSON 3

# PROBING A VERY WILLING HUMAN

I t feels good to be back in my normal clothes again. They're two strips of airy fabric with a line of beads connecting the two, crossing my belly and my back. Each of the beads tells a story and usually, I'd only wear this outfit for ceremonial occasions back on Ank, but I decided I wanted to present myself in the best possible way to our new human.

"He's waking up," A-Ven warns.

We're in our small medbay, barely big enough for the three of us. Our ship is tiny, but until now, we've not needed anything bigger. Now that we have our own human, we may have to think about upgrading.

We've taken off the male's red coat and some of the other garments he wore under it. It's crazy how many layers he had under that coat. I would have melted wearing only half of them. Now he's naked apart from bright red underpants. I've been desperate to take a peek and see if his sack really is as dangerous as the Planelyser™ said, but one of the rules of the IGU says that we shouldn't proceed too fast. Our abductee needs to feel safe and comfortable when he wakes up.

My sister waves a medscanner above the male's head and looks pleased with the results. She gives me an encouraging nod, signalling that I can start the introduction.

"Welcome to our ship," I say loudly. His eyelids

flicker open, exposing beautiful green eyes. Almost the same shade as our skin. It's destiny.

"We have abducted you, but do not fear, we will look after you and make sure you're happy. My name is A-Vay and this is my sister A-Ven. We-"

"Ho, ho, what the fuck?"

Santa's voice is deep and delicious, the kind of voice that makes shivers run down your back and makes your nipples harden with excitement. I look down and yes, all four of my nipples are erect, pushing against the fabric of my skimpy garment.

I look at A-Ven and see it's affected her the same way. The probing can't begin soon enough. I've heard stories from other IGU students that probing can develop into outright sex if done correctly. In our previous abductions, we never had such luck, but our abductees were never as hot as this one, either.

"You have been abducted," I repeat. "You are on our spaceship and we have left your solar system. We have implanted you with a translation chip which is why you're able to understand us."

"How are you feeling?" my sister asks.

"Ho, ho, cold. It's freezing in here."

"We can increase the temperature a little," I offer and command the ship to do so. "We assumed you'd like it cold, living where you do."

"Ho, ho, I would be warmer if you gave me back my coat. Why did you undress me?"

He's taking this surprisingly well. He's not even tried to get off the bed, let alone escape from the room.

By now, all our previous abductees were crying and shouting, but not this one. He's oozing confidence and calm.

"We prepared you for the probing," A-Ven explains. "We're going to take off the rest of your clothes before we proceed, but we didn't want you to wake up completely naked. It's not recommended."

"Ho, ho, recommended?"

"We're students at the Intergalactic University," I say proudly. "You're part of our final assignment before we graduate from a course in Alien Abduction. But don't worry, we've done this before. You're in safe hands. We're not amateurs."

"Ho, ho, I'm glad about that," he replies drily. Good, he's got a sense of humour. "Ho, ho, ho, I assume you want presents from me. Got to say, I've never brought something to aliens, but I always wondered if you were out there. Serving just the one planet gets boring over time. Maybe I should expand my business." He grins. "This could be the start of a wonderful partnership. My reindeer don't fly into space, believe me, I've tried. By the way, where are my loyal beasts?"

I exchange a look with my sister. He's taking this almost too well. Business? Serving? Presents? I have so many questions, but it's supposed to be us answering his questions, not the other way round. Interrogation comes after the probing, not before.

"They're still at your house," A-Ven replies. "We saw no need to take them with us."

To my surprise, Santa laughs. "Ho, ho, no need?

You'll find out soon enough. Now, what was that about probing?"

"Do you consent to being probed?" A-Ven asks. "This is purely for scientific purposes. We'll add all information we gather to the IGU's planetary database which will help with researching your species."

"Ho, ho, you'll soon realise that I'm not like other humans. But go ahead, probe away. Do you need me to strip?"

"Yes, that would be helpful. But we can also disintegrate your undergarments to make it quicker."

Santa shrugs. "Ho, ho, go ahead, I'd love to see your alien technology. I'm a bit of an old-fashioned guy myself, still relying on my reindeer, and my sleigh hasn't been upgraded in two centuries, but I do love watching *Star Trek*."

I've come across that fictional vid show while researching Peritus culture. Most of it is complete bollocks, but for a species that's barely taken the first steps towards spaceflight, it's not too bad. It was actually quite entertaining, albeit for other reasons than intended.

"I have watched that," I say, eager to make him feel at ease. This will give us bonus points for our assignment. "You'll find our probing to be a lot less painful than what I've seen in those vids."

"Ho, ho, that's reassuring. Probe away. This is the most fun I've had in years." He grins at us and points at his crotch. "Let's see your disintegration technology."

I'm starting to feel a little confused by how he's

reacting to the abduction. This is unlike anything I've ever experienced or read about in textbooks. Still, I should be grateful. This will make passing our assignment a whole lot easier.

I take a laser tool from the trolley and aim it at his underpants, setting the device to fibre disintegration. With a bright zap, the fabric disappears, giving us a view of his assets. I can't help but suck in a breath. He's massive. And his sack is indeed impressive, much larger than average, if the books about humans didn't lie.

Santa seems to enjoy our appreciative silence. "Ho, ho, ho, I bet you haven't seen a cock like this before. I'm your Christmas gift, ladies, already delivered and unwrapped. Do you want to jingle my bells?"

A-Ven takes out a measuring tape. She could do it electronically with a simple press of a button, but I know she's relishing the excuse to touch him.

"First, I'm going to take your measurements," she announces. "A-Vay, could you prepare the anal probe while I'm doing this?"

I'd much rather like to watch, but I do as she asked and get the probe ready in record speed, just in time to see her measuring the length of his cock. Her eyes widen.

"This is the length of a fully-grown Ankanis. How is this possible? Humans are smaller than us, even though you're one of the taller ones."

"Ho, ho, I told you I'm special. But I shall let you into a secret: I'm able to give myself a present once every ten years. And this was one of them. My perfect abs were another. And no matter how much gingerbread and stollen I eat, I don't lose my sixpack."

"Explain the thing about presents and gifts to me, please," I ask. "We read something about that in our research, but it never quite made sense. How can you travel around the world delivering gifts all in one night? It's not physically possible."

"Ho, ho, ho, that's a trade secret. Let's just say that time and space are relative. Space on Earth, I mean. This space, the universe, now that's an entirely different beast. I hope we can come to an agreement and go into business together. But first, let's do that anal probing. It sounds exciting."

I exchange another look with A-Ven. She's just as confused as I am.

"Turn around and lie on your front," I tell him. "I've warmed the probe so it shouldn't feel too invasive."

"Ho, ho, I love a bit of an invasion. I met this Viking lady once, many years ago, and – aaaaahhhhhhhh that feels good."

A-Ven has started inserting the probe while he was talking. His arse is perfectly formed, just like the rest of him. I wonder if this was one of his wishes, too. The shape of it lends itself to be squeezed and I can't wait to try what it feels like. For now, I stand back and simply watch as my sister slowly pushes the probe deep into his arse while Santa groans in contentment.

"Ho, ho, ho, that makes me hard like a candy cane. If you aren't careful I'll have to jingle my bells myself."

"No, I'll do that for you," I say hurriedly, earning myself a stern glance from my sister. "Can you turn on your side?"

Santa grins at me and licks his lips. Maybe I should taste him first. That could be seen as part of the probing, right? Kissing him to check if he tastes as good as he looks. Maybe he'll have the same sweet yet spicy scent as his house.

He does as I asked, rolling onto his side so that his back is towards A-Ven. His cock has grown even more in size, now bigger than that of an Ankanis. This will be a tight fit. Perfect. Moisture is collecting between my legs and I feel the first trickle of mating fluid running down my leg. My nipples are so hard that it's almost painful.

I reach out and gently wrap my hand around his cock. His skin is silky but beneath it, he's hard as a tree trunk. I squeeze my thighs together, feeling the wetness between them. I don't think I'm going to last through the entire probing process, not with his cock in sight. I slide my fingers up and down his length, feeling every thick vein beneath the surface.

Santa groans, but it could be from the anal probing. A-Ven has a dreamy look on her face as she takes measurements and moves the probe in and out. It's almost as if she's fucking him with it. I increase my pace and add my second hand, stroking him fast.

It's nothing like stroking an Ankani cock. He's harder, stronger, and I bet he will feel amazing once he's inside me. There's no if. Just when.

"Ho, ho, take it slow," Santa groans. "I've not done this in a long time. I wouldn't want to disappoint you."

A-Ven looks at me with the same incredulous expression I'm sure is displaying on my face. "I doubt you could disappoint us," I tell him, my voice hoarse with desire. I want him so much it hurts. Mating fluid is coating my thighs, showing that I'm ready for him. I don't know if humans have the same tell-tale signs of when a female is eager to mate, but if he doesn't get the message, I will have to spell it out for him. There's no way I'm leaving this room without an orgasm.

I continue stroking him with one hand and cup his sack with my other.

"Ho, ho yes, jingle my bells, baby," the male breathes, his hands grasping the edges of the bed as if he needs something to hold on to. I grin. He's in for the ride of his life.

His sack - if that's really the term humans use - is large and full. Bells, he called the two balls inside. I move them around with my fingers, eliciting noises from Santa that drive me even crazier. I need him. I want him to grunt like that while he's inside me, while I'm clenching around him.

"Can I lick your sack?" my sister suddenly asks.

"Ho, ho, ho, most definitely. Don't stop the probing, though, my little green elf."

I want to ask what an elf is, but that's when he reaches out and touches my hip. "Ho, ho, do you need to wear clothes for the probing? I'd love to see what you're hiding beneath those rags."

Did he just call my ceremonial outfit 'rags'? I should punish him for that, but in this moment, I don't care. I almost rip off my clothes, exposing my full breasts.

"Ho, ho, ho, ho," Santa gasps. "Four breasts? Christmas has come early!"

I know human females only have two, which seems not quite enough when you consider rearing a brood. Maybe they have less offspring here. Once I have babies, at least three or four at a time, I wouldn't want to be stuck with only two breasts to feed them from.

I step closer until he can touch me. He gingerly reaches out for me, touching one nipple, then the next. It's as if he's asking for permission with every small touch. I bend down to give him full access. He's still on his side and it would make it easier if he were on his back, but A-Ven still has the probe inside of him and is fucking him with hard, furious strokes. Every time she pushes in, Santa's cock jerks. I'm amazed he's not come yet with her pleasuring him with the probe and me stroking him. Although I kind of forgot about the stroking and only held him while he was inspecting my nipples. I start running my hand up and down again before an idea strikes me. I reach down and coat my fingers with my mating fluid before touching his cock again.

Santa roars when the green liquid comes into contact with his skin.

"Have I hurt you?" I ask, jumping back in shock. I'm already reaching for a cloth to wipe off the fluid when he laughs.

"Ho, ho, no, not in the slightest. I've never felt anything like it. It's like you've wrapped my cock in tinsel. So many sensations. So good. Do it again, little elf."

I add more mating fluid to my hand and gently wrap it around his cock. Santa groans deeply and sucks in a breath.

"Ho, ho, ho, I'm close. Are you ready for your presents?"

# LESSON 4

# BECOMING FAMILIAR WITH YOUR ABDUCTEE

S anta massages my sister's breasts and that's when I decide that I'm going to be the first to ride him. I'm not letting her have all the fun. Granted, probing him has made me so wet that mating fluid has run down to my ankles, but now I need to be touched.

I slowly pull out the probe - it switched itself off ages ago after measuring the same values ten times - and let it drop to the floor. I strip off as fast as I can, then nudge Santa by the hip to lie on his back. He turns to look at me and I relish when his eyes widen at the sight. Technically, my sister and I are identical, but I still think I'm the prettier one. I'm slightly more voluptuous and my curves are softer.

"Ho, ho, hot," our male mutters. "I wonder what you taste like."

I don't answer. Instead, I swing a leg over the bed so my wet pussy is above his face. A drop of mating fluid falls right onto Santa's lips, barely missing his beard. He licks it and his eyes widen, his pupils dilating. Without a word, he grabs my thighs and pulls me down. The tip of his tongue slides along my opening, licking up the mating fluid.

He sighs in delight. "Ho, ho, ho, you taste like hot, spicy mulled wine. I could drink you up in one go."

And then he pushes his tongue into me and my world explodes into stars. No male has ever done that to me before. I've missed out. Terribly. I moan as he flicks his tongue against my pleasure bud, swirling around it, then invading me once again. My thighs quiver, my pussy clenches at the sensation. It's so intense, almost better than having his cock inside me. His beard rubs against my skin, but it's soft and not scratchy at all, only adding to the wonderful feeling.

While he's drinking my mulled wine, whatever that is, he's still massaging my sister's breasts, pulling on her nipples before gently cupping her mounds with his large hands. I copy him, doing the same to myself while imagining that it's his hands on my skin. Not that I'd want to swap places with her. His tongue is showing me pleasures that I didn't know existed in this universe. I'm swaying slightly, desperate for something to hold on to.

"Ho, ho, ho, you better get ready, my tree is about to shed its snow," Santa announces, breathing hard. "Who of you is going to ride my sleigh?"

I look at A-Vay. I know we both want to be the first and I also know that neither of us is going to back down. I show her my thumb and she nods. We're going to play for the honour of receiving Santa's present. She raises her thumb too and we both count to three under our breath. As one, we throw our nail dart at each other. Mine hits her a moment before hers hits my cheek. I swipe it off, glad neither of us is poisonous. The darts beneath our thumbnails are a quirky leftover of evolution. They'll need a day to regenerate, but it's great for quick sister battles. We've done this ever since we were younglings.

Santa never saw our little exchange; his face is still buried between my legs. His tongue is working miracles and I'm very aware that I won't last much longer. Luckily, I won and I have the right to kunik with him first. With no small amount of regret, I leave my position above his head and kneel on the bed, straddling him. His cock points up straight, aiming at my opening. I'm so wet that when I lower myself onto him, he slides in with no resistance. He's large, stretching my inner walls, but it doesn't hurt. On the contrary, it feels simply amazing.

Once he's fully inside, I slowly circle my hips, getting used to the feeling of him, enjoying the blissful feeling of being filled to the brink. Santa groans and grabs my hips, nudging me to fuck him properly. I comply, guided by his grip, moving up and down his hard shaft. I close my eyes and arch my back, my entire being focused on where I merge with my male. We're one and when we reach the final cliff, we come as one. His hot seed fills me as I cry out with pleasure, my inner muscles contracting around him, milking him, extracting every last drop. He's given me my present, just like he said, and it's wonderful.

The bed isn't wide enough for me to lie next to him like I'd want to, so I move to a chair, still floating in that dreamy state of bliss. I watch as A-Vay takes my place, taking Santa on a wild ride, her breasts jumping up and down, her moans mixing with his breathy groans.

He shows no signs of needing a break. He fucks her as passionately as he did with me, grinding his hips against hers, pushing his cock deep inside. It's such a turn on watching them together. Without thinking, I touch myself, pushing a finger inside of me, refreshing the echo of Santa's cock that I can still feel in my dripping pussy.

A-Vay and Santa seem close to their climax, and so am I, quivering on the edge, just about holding on, but I wait until they come with wild shouts of ecstasy before I allow myself to come, squirming on my chair, almost unbearably happy that we abducted this male.

# LESSON 5

# DEALING WITH STOWAWAYS

Santa follows me to the cargo bay. He's put on clothes again, lots of them, complaining that our ship is too cold. He's suggested that we could increase the temperature and that my sister and I could walk around naked to make up for it. I'm tempted. After the ride I just had, any opportunity to tempt our male is appreciated. There's no way I'm going to bed tonight without another mating.

We got an alert of life signs suddenly appearing in the cargo bay just when we'd recovered from our passionate kunik. Bad timing, but it could have been worse.

As soon as the door to the cargo bay opens, a musky scent hits my nose. I squeeze my nostrils shut, blocking out the smell. Inside the otherwise empty room stand four reindeer, all of them staring at us from large, brown eyes. They're the same beasts as back on Peritus, although while there they matched the cold, snowy landscape, here they stand out so much that I can't help but laugh. Animals on my ship. We've never had that before. A-Ven and I occasionally transport animal products like eggs and wool, but we've always refused to have live animals on board. They make a mess, stink and someone needs to clean up their poo.

Santa approaches his reindeer and they immediately crowd him from all sides, nuzzling him with their steaming muzzles while making strange honking sounds.

"Ho, ho, ho, there you are. I knew you'd follow me," Santa cheers and strokes the beasts.

I stay close to the door, not quite comfortable being near those formidable animals. I may be taller than them, but their antlers look ferocious. They could easily skewer me.

"Ho, ho, my green elf, come meet my reindeer," my abductee invites me and beckons me closer. "They're eager to say hello. This is Mistletoe, the small one is Sparkle, to my right is Baubles and the one that's about to lick your face is Icicle. Watch out, if he claims you, he won't let go of you for days. He's very possessive, aren't you, boy?"

I retreat to the wall, away from the slobbering reindeer that's approaching me. Licking my face? I don't think so. Who knows what germs are in that beast's saliva.

"How did they get here?" I ask. "The airlock never opened. We would have had to approve that. Besides, it's not like they could have flown through the vacuum of space. And they definitely didn't board our ship back on Peritus. The life signs didn't appear until just now."

Santa shrugs. "Ho, ho, my reindeer have a magic of their own. It's good that they're here now. It would have been bad for my reputation to show up without them. It's bad enough that I no longer have my sleigh, but-"

"We have your sleigh!" I interrupt. "We used it to transport you to the ship. It's in the room next door."

"Ho, ho, ho! I could kiss you, elfie!"

I grin at him. "Do it, don't hold back."

Within an instant, he's upon me. His strong arms wrap around my waist and he pulls me close until all I can see is him, his beard, his stunning eyes. His lips meet mine in a passionate kiss that's nothing like I've ever experienced. He tastes sweet yet spicy, hot yet pleasantly cold. Our tongues dance in tune to music only we can hear.

Santa pushes me against the wall and without thinking, I wrap my legs around his waist. I'm taller than him, but he's strong enough to hold me. I grind against his cock which is hard against the various layers of his clothing. I wish he was naked.

A reindeer honks, destroying the moment. Santa chuckles and slowly breaks the kiss, ending with one last swipe of his tongue against my lips. Cool air hits my wet lips and for the first time, I feel cold in my own ship. I want him touching me again.

"Ho, ho, ho, later, my delicious four-breasted elf," Santa whispers hoarsely. "I will make sure both of us will end up on the naughty list tonight. But now we should discuss business."

"Business?"

My mind is muddled from our kiss. I couldn't think of anything I'd like to do less than talk about something as mundane as business. Besides, it's not part of our Alien Abduction course. Next up should be *Seduction*

*Techniques for Inexperienced Aliens*, followed by *The Mating Habits of Humans* before proceeding to *Beard Care for Beginners*. We designed that module ourselves after seeing how much facial hair our abduction target possessed.

I suppose we've already covered seduction and mating in a very practical way. We'll just have to write up a report for Professor Katila so that it counts for our assignment. It might be embarrassing to describe in detail what we did with Santa, but after reading previous students' assignments, our experience was very tame. There were no tentacles or thorns involved, not even a tail. Compared to other species, both human and Ankani physiology is really quite boring.

I sigh and turn to the reindeer again. "What kind of food do they need? I doubt we have anything suitable on board."

"Ho, ho, they prefer a diet of cotton candy and chocolate-covered apples with the occasional nibble on my gingerbread house. However, they will survive on hay."

"We'll have to stop by the nearest space station and buy some food for them."

"Ho, ho, excellent. We can start our business venture there."

"Business?" A-Ven asks, stepping through the open door behind me. "What are you two plotting?"

I shrug. "I'm not quite sure, but I hope it involves lots of mating."

Santa laughs, making his entire beard shake. "Ho,

ho, hottie, you're truly insatiable. You're definitely going on my naughty list and I will make sure you stay on it.

"Do you really have to start every sentence with 'ho, ho'?" my sister asks.

"Ho, ho, yes, it's a speech impediment that I was born with. It can get a little annoying, but I'm used to it. By now, humans would be disappointed if I didn't do it. Ho, ho, ho!"

I smile at him. "It's kind of hot, especially earlier when you came..."

A-Ven grins. "Indeed. Let's not stop with the ho-ing. But what's that business you want to discuss?"

Santa points at his reindeer. "Ho, ho, every year I travel across the world and deliver presents to children. They send me their wish lists, but most of the time I ignore those and simply give them what their parents requested. Easier that way, you understand? Besides, it's pretty hard giving world peace to children just because they want it. That's way above my pay grade.

"I've done this for so long that I've grown tired of always travelling the same route. I've changed it up, visited countries in random orders, but in the end, it's always the same. And with time, it's grown boring. They no longer build houses with proper chimneys that I can climb down. Now that was a challenge, back in the days! Now, I have to leave the presents on their doorstep or have to sneak into their houses. Dull. I've been looking for a new challenge and you ladies have given me just that. I'm going to extend my present delivery business to all of space, one planet at a time. You shall be my high-tech sleigh, transporting me to where I'm needed. Once I'm on solid ground, I can use my reindeer and sleigh to do the actual deliveries. We'll split the fees."

"Fees?" I ask. "Who pays you for doing this?"

"Ho, ho, automatic affiliate payments. Whenever I deliver toys, their manufacturers pay me a fee for it. Not that they know, of course. It disappears from their bank accounts without them realising. They usually put it down to fraud if they notice, but that's rare. I don't get a lot, but if you deliver presents to billions of children, it quickly adds up."

A-Ven whistles appreciatively. "I'm impressed. You must be loaded if you've done this for centuries."

Santa gives us a good-natured smile. "Ho, ho, definitely. I don't have much use for it, though. I mostly spend it on treating my reindeer."

"I like your plan," I admit. "But you may not be aware that Christmas is a Peritus thing. It's not celebrated on other planets."

"Ho, ho, Peritus?"

"The official intergalactic name for your planet."

"Ho, ho, huh. I wonder why anyone bothered giving it a new name."

A-Ven laughs. "It's not a new name. It was called Peritus before life appeared and it was just a boiling rock. Once you officially have first contact, your fellow humans will be told the name and will hopefully start using it. It'll make things much easier for intergalactic cooperation if everyone uses the same terminology."

"Ho, ho, interesting." He turns to me. "I don't share your concerns about Christmas. If the locals don't know it, they will still be happy about receiving gifts. I might be able to amend my branding a little, make it more universal." Santa laughs. "Universal. Get it?"

I look at A-Ven and shrug. Some things get lost in translation, that's for sure, even with our advanced technology.

"We have a festival called Ma-Tan," I muse. "We give presents to both our younglings and elders in celebration of life itself. There is no one person who delivers those gifts, though. We do it for each other and take credit for it."

"Oh yes," my sister adds with a grin. "And it's important to thank everyone who gave you something individually. Entire family feuds have started because no proper thanks was given during Ma-Tan."

"Ho, ho, I can work with that. Does that mean you're up for it? Becoming my elves, joining my business?"

I point at the reindeer. "Only if you deal with their waste."

A-Ven laughs. "And we demand daily probing and mating. To keep you in shape. We wouldn't want you to get out of breath during your deliveries."

Santa's eyes sparkle as he wraps an arm around each of us and pulls us close. "Ho, ho, ho, I wouldn't dream of refusing. And I believe I'm ready for you to jingle my bells once again..."

# LESSON 6

~~BEARD CARE~~

~~FOR BEGINNERS~~

## Final grades!

The green clouds of Ank cover most of our planet's atmosphere, hiding it from view, but that doesn't stop the warm feeling of *home* spreading in my chest. I stare through the porthole, glad to be home.

After a brief stop at Kitt-Y-6, the closest space station to Peritus, we headed straight for Ank to start our first Christmas mission. I'm excited to be Santa's elf. He's explained the function of an elf to us and there's nothing I love more than helping him deliver his gifts – especially if he's delivering them deep inside of me.

We've got enough food for the reindeer to last us several months, but we're hoping they will change their diet to plants we can find on Ank. That will lower our costs substantially. Buying hay in space is the most expensive thing I've ever done.

Before we set foot on our home planet, however, we've got one last thing to do. I don't want to step before our nestfeeders without our IGU certificate.

"It's time," A-Vay announces just before Professor Katila appears on our screen.

Her three eyes stare at us with the same piercing gaze as always, but her purple lips are curved into a smile.

"A-Vay, A-Ven," she greets us. "It's a pleasure to see you. And this must be Santa?"

"Ho, ho, help, I've been abducted by aliens!" Santa calls out, grinning widely. "Please don't take me back to my planet."

The professor chuckles. "I see your abductee has quickly got used to life away from Peritus. Are they treating you well?"

"Ho, ho, ho, most definitely. I couldn't have asked for better abductors."

Santa gives me a wink. Professor Katila is blissfully unaware that we mated just a few minutes ago before reaching Ank's orbit. Mating fluid still coats my thighs, but luckily the screen only shows us from the shoulders up. It's kind of ho-ho-hot, knowing that Santa's seed is still within me.

"That is good to hear," our teacher says before turning her attention back on us. Her middle eye is fixed on A-Vay while her lower two eyes focus on me. "I have read your assignment and after discussing it with my colleagues, I've decided on a grade. Since this was your final assignment, I can now tell you the final grade for your Alien Abduction for Beginners course."

She pauses for dramatic effect, but I resist the urge to tell her to hurry up.

"First, your assignment. While your probing was a little unorthodox and you skipped several introductory sessions with your abductee, I agree that in your situation this was the best course of action. Your abductee was clearly happy with his abduction and you therefore didn't require any of the practices outlined in

*Dealing with an Angry Human.* I've decided to award you nine out of ten IGU credits for this assignment, meaning your final grade is an Alpha Star. Congratulations, you're the best students this year."

I look at A-Vay with delight. I knew we'd be good, but an Alpha Star is more than I'd hoped for. Our nestfeeders will be so proud. They were satisfied with our choice to become traders, but having not just one but two qualified abductors in the family will increase their standing in the community.

"I'm going to message you your certificate in a moment," the Professor continues. "Usually, I'd invite you to apply for the Alien Abduction for Professionals class, but from what I've read in your assignment, you'll be kept busy by your abductee, in more way than one."

She winks at us with all three eyes before the screen turns black.

I never thought our stern teacher had a sense of humour.

A second later, a message appears in our inbox. I open it and have it appear in the holo projector so that the other two can read it at the same time. It's our IGU certificate, signed by both Professor Katila and Professor Z, the university's headmaster.

"Now it's official," my sister mutters. "We're professional abductors."

"Ho, ho, ho, if you dare to abduct anyone else I will remove you from my naughty list," Santa warns. "No more jingling bells, no more licking my candy cane."

"No abductions," I say quickly. "You're enough for us, don't worry."

"Ho, ho, good. I will keep you satisfied, don't worry. I may be old in years, but I have more stamina than my reindeer put together. My Christmas tree won't grow limp any time soon, not with you two around."

He gets up and walks towards the porthole to look down at Ank. Our home. For at least some time, it will be Santa's home too. We're going to explore the planet together, delivering presents, making people happy. Plus having lots and lots of sex.

"Time to start the landing sequence," A-Vay says and turns to the controls. "We don't want to be late for dinner."

I let her take over and sit on Santa's lap. He wraps his arms around my waist and kisses the nape of my neck.

"Merry Christmas," he whispers and puts his hands on my breasts, jingling my bells just the way I like it. "Ho, ho, ho."

*Do you have what it takes to abduct an alien? Take this test to find out – and get your own IGU certificate!*
https://hi.switchy.io/AAFBtest

*This isn't the only story set in this world.*
*Start the series with* Alien Abduction for Beginners

*(reverse harem romance) or how about some space pirates in* Alien Abduction for Pirates *(m/f romance)? Flick the page for a full list of IGU books!*

*Subscribe to Skye's newsletter for all the latest books and updates: skyemackinnon.com/newsletter*

# COULD YOU ABDUCT A HUMAN?

Do you think you've got what it takes to become an alien abductor? Take this test to find out!
**skyemackinnon.com/alien-abduction-test**

*(if you share your results on social media, be sure to tag me)*

And if you feel like you've passed this course, you can download a certificate!
**hi.switchy.io/AAFBcertificate**

Abductions aren't easy - which is exactly why the Intergalactic University offers a range of courses at various levels. Immerse yourself in this strange, comical universe and work on your abduction skills.

**Find all books in this series here:**

skyemackinnon.com/intergalactic-guide

Alien Abduction for Beginners

Alien Abduction for Professionals

Alien Abduction for Experts

*(reverse harem/why choose trilogy, to be read in order)*

Alien Abduction for Santa

*(fmf standalone)*

Alien Abduction for Pirates

*(mf standalone)*

Alien Abduction for Milkmen

*(mm standalone)*

Alien Abduction for Unicorns

*(mf standalone)*

THE STARLIGHT UNIVERSE

*This book is part of the Starlight Universe, an entire galaxy filled with hunky aliens, exotic planets, and the human women ready to find love among the stars.*

## Starlight Highlanders Mail Order Brides

Alien Highlanders in kilts come to Earth in search of brides... and take them to planet Albya. Three m/f standalones full of humour, action and steamy romance. Part of the Intergalactic Dating Agency.

## The Intergalactic Guide to Humans

A humorous take on alien abductions, probing and other shenanigans. One reverse harem trilogy about clueless aliens and the human woman they abducted, followed by several standalone romances with various pairings (m/f, f/m/f and m/m). If you want light entertainment filled with unicorns, fabulous misunderstandings and unusual body parts, this is the series for you.

## Starlight Vikings

Set on Earth and on the spaceship Valkyr, this trilogy of m/f standalones is all about hunky alien Vikings in need of females. Part of the Intergalactic Dating Agency.

## Starlight Monsters

These aliens are not your usual humanoids... they have claws, fangs, tails, scales, knotty dicks and will growl at you. Interconnected m/f standalones with lots of action, steam and fated mates.

# ABOUT THE AUTHOR

Skye MacKinnon is a Scottish romance author who was raised by elves in the mystical Highlands and calls the Loch Ness monster her friend. Her bestselling books weave together romance with action, suspense and whimsical humour, creating page-turners filled with strong heroines, alpha heroes and loveable monsters.

Whether she's writing about aliens in kilts, hunky Vikings or cat shifter assassins, Skye likes to put a new spin on familiar tropes. Some of her heroines don't have to choose, some fall in love with other women, and others get abducted by clueless aliens.

Skye lives with her bossy cat on the west coast of Scotland and uses the dramatic views from her office as an inspiration, no matter whether she writes fantasy, paranormal or science fiction romance. Until she gets abducted by aliens, that is.

Subscribe to her newsletter:

**skyemackinnon.com/newsletter**

Find all of Skye's books on her website, skyemackinnon.com, where you can also order signed paperbacks and swag. Many of her books are available as audiobooks.

PARANORMAL & FANTASY ROMANCE

- **Claiming Her Bears** (post-apocalyptic shifter reverse harem)
- **Daughter of Winter** (fantasy reverse harem)
- **Catnip Assassins** (urban fantasy reverse harem)
- **Infernal Descent** (paranormal reverse harem based on Dante's Inferno, co-written with Bea Paige)
- **Seven Wardens** (fantasy reverse harem co-written with Laura Greenwood)
- **The Lost Siren** (post-apocalyptic, paranormal reverse harem co-written with Liza Street)

- **Starlight Highlanders Mail Order Brides** (sci-fi m/f romance, part of the Intergalactic Dating Agency)
- **Starlight Vikings** (sci-fi m/f romance, part of the Intergalactic Dating Agency)
- **Starlight Monsters** (m/f romance)
- **The Intergalactic Guide to Humans** (sci-fi romance with various pairings)
- **Between Rebels** (sci-fi reverse harem set in the Planet Athion shared world)
- **The Mars Diaries** (sci-fi reverse harem)
- **Through the Gates** (dystopian reverse harem co-written with Rebecca Royce)
- **Aliens and Animals** (f/f sci-fi romance co-written with Arizona Tape)



- **Academy of Time** (time travel academy standalones, reverse harem and m/f)
- **Defiance** (contemporary reverse harem with a hint of thriller/suspense)



- Song of Souls – m/f fantasy romance, fairy tale retelling
- Wings of Time and Fate - YA fantasy

- Their Hybrid – steampunk reverse harem
- Partridge in the P.E.A.R. - sci-fi reverse harem co-written with Arizona Tape
- Highland Butterflies – lesbian romance

## BOX SETS

- Daggers & Destiny – a Skye MacKinnon starter library
- Stars & Seduction - a Sci-Fi Romance starter library